For Mary, Malcolm and Tom Glenister,
in loving memory of Alice
S.G.

Visit Sally Grindley's website: www.sallygrindley.co.uk

ORCHARD BOOKS
96 Leonard Street, London EC2A 4XD
Orchard Books Australia
32/45-51 Huntley Street, Alexandria, NSW 2015
ISBN 1 84362 303 0 (hardback)
ISBN 1 84362 382 X (paperback)
First published in Great Britain in 2004
First paperback publication in 2005
Text © Sally Grindley 2004
Illustrations © Tony Ross 2004
The rights of Sally Grindley to be identified as the author and of Tony Ross
to be identified as the illustrator of this work have been asserted by them
in accordance with the Copyright, Designs and Patents Act, 1988.
A CIP catalogue record for this book is available from the British Library.
1 3 5 7 9 10 8 6 4 2 (hardback)
1 3 5 7 9 10 8 6 4 2 (paperback)
Printed in Great Britain

ABOUT THE AUTHOR

D.J. Lucas

always wanted to be a writer. Today D.J. is one of
the most popular children's authors around.
D.J.'s books include *My Teacher's a Nutcase*,
winner of the Smartstart Award and *I Dare You*,
winner of the Bitread Book Award.

Sally Grindley

the acclaimed children's writer, is D.J.'s favourite
author. Sally Grindley says, 'I would do anything
to write as well as D.J. Lucas, even lock myself in
a cupboard with NO biscuits to eat!'

Dear Max

BY D.J. LUCAS
AKA SALLY GRINDLEY

ORCHARD BOOKS

To my friend Max

D.J.

10th January

Dear D.J.Lucas,

My uncle bought me one of your books for
Christmas. It's called *Who's Afraid of the Big Bad
Boy?*. I really like it. I like it most because the
little girl turns out to be a big hero. Is it your
best book?

Have you written any other books?

I want to be a writer when I grow up.

Love from Max
Age 9

19th January

Dear Max,

Thank you for your letter. I'm so glad you like
Who's Afraid of the Big Bad Boy?. I couldn't
have the bully winning, could I?

I have written quite a few books. I think it was
thirty-five at the last count, and I'm about to
start work on a new one. My best-known titles
are *I Dare You, Not on
my Patch, My Teacher's
a Nutcase, Cornflakes
Forever* and *Give me
Back my Boomerang*.

Best wishes,

D.J.Lucas

Dear D. J. Lucas,

Thirty-five books is a lot! My mum says we can have a look for your books in the library next time we go.

My teacher Mr Peabody (I call him Beanbrain) says he's heard of you. I showed him my book, *Who's Afraid of the Big Bad Boy?*, and he said he hadn't read it so I told him what it was about and he thought it sounded good. I told him it was the best book I have ever read and he said he would have to read it some time, but then he told me to sit down because we were going to write about what we did at Christmas.

I didn't want to write about what I did at Christmas because it's me and my mum's saddest time, even though we try very hard not to let it be.

Do you like writing books?

Love from Max again
Age 9

I'm glad you didn't have the big bully winning, but sometimes they do. Hugo Broadbent in my class is a bully. I call him Hugo Broadbottom but not to his face.

28th January

Dear/Max again,

I do enjoy writing most of the time.
Sometimes, though, my imagination deserts
me. I sit there and stare at my blank piece of
paper thinking, what the chicken drumsticks
am I going to write about now? Sometimes a
whole day goes by and I'm still there with my
blank piece of paper, shorter nails, and a lot
of empty coffee mugs. At times like that, I do
not enjoy being a writer in the slightest. In
fact, I'd rather be a trout fisherman!

Happily, every now and again a brilliant idea
springs into my mind. I snatch it quickly and
soon find my blank piece of paper is covered

with words, some of which seem to have arrived there by magic. Hey Presto!

I hope the shelves of your library are stacked high with my books!

Happy reading, Max,

D.J. Lucas

Dear D. J. Lucas,

We went to the library and found fifteen of
your books. I asked the librarian why the shelves
weren't stacked high with them because you're
the best, and she said that they come in and out
all the time because people keep borrowing
them. I borrowed *Cornflakes Forever*. My best
friend, Jenny, thinks that's a silly name for a book,
but I think it's funny. I've only read five pages so
far, but I like the idea that Timothy always refuses
to eat anything except cornflakes. What's going
to happen to him? Mum says I'm like

Timothy because I
always want to have
ketchup. I wouldn't want it on my cornflakes
though! She says that my dad was just as bad
because he always wanted mustard. **UGH!**

I'd like to write a story, but I don't know where to start. I want it to be good and funny and have lots happening and brillypants characters. Please will you help me?

Love from your friend Max

6th February

Hello friend Max,

I shall have to buy some more writing paper!

Well, we're both in the same boat. I've been asked by my editor to write a new book for older children, and you want to write a story. Do you have any idea what you want to write about? I certainly don't. This is one of those times when my imagination has left me completely stranded.

If you're stuck as well, Max, why don't we both decide what interests us most at the moment and start there? What about animals? Pirates? Monsters? Children? Animals are always a good subject because there are lots of different sorts and they do lots of different things. In fact, you can make them do anything you like, really.

I liked the picture of you at the bottom of your letter. Here's a photograph (bad) of my dog, Ambush, and my cat, Donut. Ambush is a nutty mutt, the daftest dog anyone has ever met. He's called Ambush because when he was a pup he used to jump at anything that moved, especially Donut.

I hope that by now you've discovered what happens to Cornflake Timothy.

Happy writing,

D.J.Lucas

Ambush

Donut

Dear D.J. Lucas,

It's me, Max, again.

I've decided to write about a tiny little bear because I've just watched a programme about bears. Did you know there's a bear called a spectacle bear because he's got rings round his eyes that make him look as if he's wearing glasses? I'm going to give my bear spectacles and I'm going to call him Grizzle.
This is what he looks like. What are you going to write about for your book?

I wish I could have a nutty mutt, but Mum says I can't because we live in a flat and we're not allowed pets. And she says that it wouldn't be fair because when she's at work and I'm at school there wouldn't be anyone to look after it. My Uncle Derek has just bought a Saluki. I thought he had bought a motorbike until Mum told me I was thinking of a Suzuki! Have you ever heard of a dog called a Saluki? Uncle Derek says it's a type of greyhound. I can't wait to go round and see it, but a Suzuki would have been even better.

Has Donut got a hole in the middle, or is she full of jam? Do you like the name of my bear? Mum says to grizzle is whining and crying a lot so I think my bear will cry all the time – **BOO-HOO!** – because he's a sad bear. Also there's a type of bear called a grizzly, but I expect you know that.

What shall I do next?

Thank you for writing to me.

Love, Max

This is a picture of Donut
with a hole in the middle.
I've got to the bit in
'Cornflakes for Forever' where
Timothy enters a Cornflake
Eating Marathon. I hope he wins.

16th February

Dear Max,

I think Grizzle is a great name for a bear.
Why is he sad? Does he have sore feet?
Does he keep running out of honey? Do
coconuts keep falling on his head? Does he
have ants in his pants? Is someone being
horrible to him? Perhaps he hasn't got many
friends.

I like your drawing. The spectacles make
Grizzle look extremely intelligent. What
about doing another picture of Grizzle
showing where he lives and what sort of
things he has around him? That might
help your story.

I used to have a Suzuki, but I wasn't very good at staying on it. I would find it easier to stay on a Saluki.

I'm afraid I still haven't started my new book, but my imagination is working on it. I'm mulling over lots of different ideas at the moment.

Best wishes,

D.J.Lucas

Dear D. J. Lucas,

I've finished reading *Cornflakes Forever*. I think
it's really funny at the end when Timothy starts
 eating baked beans instead. I told
Beanbrain about it and he said he
would have to read it some time
too, but I bet he doesn't. Hugo Broadbottom
said it sounded stupid, but I don't care what
he thinks.

Mum says I shouldn't pester you because
that might be why you haven't started your
book yet. My best friend Jenny at school
says she's never heard of you and that you
can't be very good if you can't think of
anything to write about. We had a big
argument because I said that you had

millions of ideas and that was why it was taking you so long to get started because you had to choose which one was the best.

Two hours later! Mum's just taken me for a walk by a river. I think it's going to be where Grizzle lives. This is a picture of him catching fish because bears do catch fish, I saw it on the programme I watched. They're very clever. They wait for a fish to jump then grab it in their paws.

I've just had a brillypants idea. Grizzle is going to be rubbish at catching fish because he's so tiny and that's why he

grizzles. Every time he catches a fish it
leaps out of his paws and back into the
water – **BOO-HOO**!

Love, Max

Are you very famous? I can't
believe you used to ride a
motorbike. I didn't think
writers rode motorbikes.
I'm going to see Uncle Derek's
Saluki tomorrow.

Dear D. J. Lucas,

Two letters in a row!

You should see Uncle Derek's Saluki.
She's only six weeks old and she's
crazy. She's already chewed a pair
of Uncle's boxer shorts to pieces,
and she weed in his walking boots!
She runs round and round in circles
chasing her tail and growling at it. I don't think
she knows it belongs to her. When we tried
to play football in Uncle's garden, she kept
running away with the ball. Uncle's going to
call her Scallywag.

My mum thinks Uncle has landed himself with
a big bundle of trouble and before I could even

ask she said, 'No, Max, you're not having one.'
So I said, 'I could have a hamster though, couldn't
I, Mum? They don't wee in people's boots.' She
groaned but I think she might give in soon. I'm
sure she'd like a
hamster. It would
make her laugh.

I bet you still haven't started your book.

Love, Max

27th February

Dear Max,

You have been busy! I like the idea of tiny Grizzle being hopeless at catching fish. Who else is going to be in your story? It's very difficult to write a good story with only one character.

I am quite famous for my books, I suppose, though I don't feel as if I am. I was once asked for my autograph in a supermarket. That was quite embarrassing. I was at the checkout when a woman thrust a piece of paper in front of me, said her son thought I was the best author on the planet, and asked me to write a special message to him. There was a big queue building up behind me and people were beginning to mutter. I ended up getting in such a flap that I nearly spelt my own name wrong.

I've been on the radio several times and on television once, but that's all. Really, my books are more famous than I am.

I haven't quite started my new book yet, but something else is brewing, something is definitely brewing.

Best wishes, D.J.

Dear D.J.Lucas,

I can't believe you've been on telly! I wish I'd seen you. Was it a long time ago?

There's a new boy in my class called Ben and he's read one of your books! He comes from Jamaica and he bought *I Dare You* at the airport in Jamaica. I bet you didn't know they sold your books in an airport in Jamaica. Anyway Ben says it's his best book and he's going to lend it to me if I promise to give it back.

Ben on the plane.

I'm going to have a really nasty horrible revolting crocodile called Crunch in my story. He's going to sit in the water and splash his tail to frighten the fish away. Grizzle can't stop him because he is too small and Crunch is too big and mean. Mum says bears and crocodiles don't live in the same place, but they're going to in my story. And I'm going to have a horrid old wolf called Snigger who hangs around with Crunch and howls with laughter every time Grizzle misses a fish. This is a picture of Snigger laughing.

hee
hee
hee

Grizzle lost his mother so he hasn't been able to learn lots of things from her. That's why he's rubbish at catching fish. Mum says if my dad was around I would have learnt lots of things from him. I learnt that polar bears live in the Arctic not the Antarctic from my dad.

Love, Max

Have you got any children?

11th March

Dear Max,

Crunch and Snigger are great characters and they're great names. Choosing the right names is one of the most difficult things in story-writing. If I'm not completely satisfied with my names, I find I can't write my story.

Crunch and Snigger will have to come in near the beginning of your story, won't they, because they're part of the reason Grizzle is so sad?

But is Grizzle going to be happy at the end of your story? I hope so! If he is, what's going to happen to make him happy? That's what you've got to think about next, and then you'll have the middle of your story. Hey Presto!

I was thrilled to hear that your friend Ben bought *I Dare You* at the airport in Jamaica. He must be a boy of remarkably good taste to have picked out my book from all the others!

I don't have any children, Max. There's just me, Ambush and Donut. I do have plenty of friends though, and I have a very special friend called Christopher whom I see as often as I can. He's a pilot, and I met him on a plane!

Best wishes,
D.J.

P.S. I was on television last year, on a rather serious programme about books. I haven't been on a chat show or anything glamorous like that.

P.P.S. I'm supposed to be getting on with my new book, but instead (or as well as!) I think I'm going to write a short story about a boy with a big imagination.

Dear D.J.Lucas,

I can't believe your friend Christopher is a pilot.
WOW! I expect he's away a lot like my Uncle

Derek. My Uncle Derek
is a lorry driver and he
drives all over the
country. His new

girlfriend Pauline misses him when he's away, like
my mum misses my dad, except my dad's never
coming back. I wish he could come back.

At least my mum's got me,
and she calls me her
little treasure and
I say, 'Not so
much of the
little, Mother, if
you please'.

our flats

My special friend is Jenny. She lives in the same block of flats as me and goes to my school.

What's the boy in your short story going to be called and what will he look like and how old will he be and will he be small or very tall? Will you call him Max like me? Please, please, treble please. It's a good name, isn't it?

I don't know if my Grizzle story is going to have a happy ending because I don't know how to make him happy, unless he grows big and that will take ages.

I've got to go now to a hospital appointment. *Again*. Boring, boring, *boring*. I've got this consultant called Mr Drew (you'll never guess what I call him!) who wears glasses on the end of his nose and peers over the top of them as if he's looking at a strange insect. Me! There's a nurse who's my friend. Her name's Trudi. She told me it was short for  Ermintrude, but I don't believe her. She calls me Sir Maximilian.

Love, Max

What does P.S. mean? And what does the D.J. in D.J. Lucas stand for? It makes you sound like you're a disc jockey, but I don't think you can be a writer and a disc jockey.

21st March

Dear Sir Maximilian,

Since you asked so nicely, and because it's a
fantastically good name, I will call my boy
Max, and he's going to be nine years old.
Shall I make him tall or short or somewhere
in between? Has he got dark hair or fair hair?
You can choose. I think he's definitely got a
huge imagination.

I hope your hospital appointment wasn't
too boring and that you're all right. I hate
going to the doctor's because I'm scared
of needles and can't stand the sight of
blood. Show me a needle and I faint
clean away.

I'm sure you're braver than that.

Best wishes,
D.J.

P.S. P.S. stands for '*post scriptum*', which is Latin. It's something you write in a letter after you have signed off. It's like an afterthought, or something you forgot to mention in the main part of your letter.

P.P.S. (*post post scriptum*!) D.J. = Daphne Jane, but don't tell anyone! You can call me D.J. if you like.

Dear D.J.,

WOW! I thought you were a man! I never
thought you would be a girl, especially since
you used to ride a motorbike. D.J. sounds like
a man. Ben thought you were a man too. Jenny
thought you would be a girl, even though she
had never heard of you.

Thank you, thank you, thank you for calling your
boy Max. He's got to be very short like me
and have fair hair. What's Max going to do in
your story?

I don't want to talk about the hospital. I've got
to have more tests next month, but it never
makes any difference. They just mess around
with me but they never make me better.

Jenny wants to write to you, but I told her she couldn't because you wouldn't have time to write to both of us and I wrote to you first and I'm the one who wants to be a writer. Jenny was a bit funny with me for a while but we're friends again now. She says she doesn't like writing letters anyway because email's better, but I haven't got email and I like to do drawings on my letters which I wouldn't be able to do on email.

Do you get lots of letters from children who read your books, and do you answer them all?

I've made up some more characters for my story. There's Grab who's a heron who keeps pecking at Grizzle like he's some kind of insect.

There's Bellow who's a great big fat hippo who
hides under the water then throws up her head,
bellows, and makes Grizzle jump. There's Creepy
the witch and I'm going to make up some more
as well.

This is a long letter compared to yours. Do you
think I'm better at writing letters than you?

Love, Max

Dear D.J,

I forgot to tell you, Creepy is a wicked witch.
She can't keep her long pointy
nose out of anyone's story.
She's going to turn the
river water pink, and
that's going to make
Grizzle's fur go all
pink so that Snigger
laughs at him even
more. I haven't decided
what to do with Snigger
yet, but he's going to come
to a very sticky end.

If you're stuck (tee hee!), why don't you have
Creepy in your story too? I don't mind, though

my Uncle Derek said I was a bit cheeky to offer
my characters to a professional author. I thought
Creepy could make the boy's imagination go
all wonky donkey.

Love, Max

P.S. I hate Hugo Broadbottom. People can't help
being small.

2nd April

Dear Max,

Goodness – you *have* been working hard on your characters! I love the idea of Bellow the big-mouthed hippo. Have you thought about having a nice character to help Grizzle? He's a bit outnumbered by baddies at the moment, poor bear.

Huge Bigbottom sounds like all your baddies rolled into one!

I don't know yet what Max is going to do in my short story but, yes, Sir Maximilian, I will make him short with fair hair.

Children do quite often write to me about my books, and I try to answer all of their letters. But you're the only one I've written to more than once. Perhaps it's because I think you're a bit special. And I think it's much more exciting to receive letters than emails, because they plop through your letterbox when you're not expecting them.

I'm afraid I must stop now. I'm going to sign some of my books in a shop miles away. I shall be very embarrassed if nobody turns up. I might just have to go and hide in a cupboard!

Love, D.J.

P.S. I think I'll leave Creepy out of my story. She sounds like big trouble to me!

Dear D.J,

HUGE BIGBOTTOM! Why didn't I think of that?! Ha, ha, I wish I had the nerve to say it to his face.

I hope you didn't have to hide in a cupboard. I would turn up if you came to a bookshop in our town. Will you come one day? I hid in a cupboard at school once when Huge Bigbottom and his pals were being horrible to me. It was where they keep the toilet rolls and soap. I've never seen so many toilet rolls. At least being small makes it easier to find good places to hide. The caretaker wasn't very happy though when he found me because I ate a biscuit that was meant for his lunch.

Love, Max

15th April

Dear Max,

You'll be pleased to know that I didn't have
to hide in a cupboard. I signed books for fifty
children and ten adults, which is sort of all
right since it was only a small town. One little
girl threw her arms round my legs and said I
was her best friend in all the world because
we were both wearing red shoes!

One day, who knows, I might visit a bookshop
near you. The trouble is that you live a long way
away. I don't usually travel more than 100 miles
from home, because it would mean leaving
Ambush and Donut on their own for too long.

Love, D.J.

Dear D.J.,

Jenny says you can't be very famous if only fifty children and ten adults came to see you. I told her it was only a small town and that probably the bookshop people didn't tell anyone you were going to be there, but she said that was just excuses. Ben tried to tell her that you *are* famous, but she laughed and said why would anyone famous want to write to me. I don't think Jenny likes me any more. She likes Huge Bigbottom.

I've got to go to hospital again tomorrow. I expect Mr Poo will say, 'Ah, now, Max isn't it?' just like he always does (even though he knows it's me).

Then he'll say, 'And how are we today, Max?' and then he'll prod and poke me. I'll feel like saying, 'We're fed up. Completely, completely, completely fed up. So there!' But Mum will give me one of her looks, so instead I'll say, 'All right, thank you', even if I'm not.

Love, Max

23rd April

Dear Max,

I'm sorry you're having a bad time at the moment. I'm sure Jenny is just a bit jealous, that's all.

I've got some news for you, Max. I'm training to do a sponsored parachute jump for charity. I am actually going to throw myself out of a plane! It's Christopher's fault. He's jumped several times and he's persuaded me to do it. Aargh! I was thinking about making myself look really brave by reading a book on the way down, even though I shall be scared out of my wits.

How's your story coming along? I've decided

that Max in my story might find school a bit difficult sometimes. Some mornings he doesn't want to go to school at all. What do you think?

Love, D.J.

Dear D.J.,

A parachute jump! I can't believe it! I told Jenny because I want her to be my friend still, but she says she thinks you're cookie. I think you're cool, so does Ben. I didn't think writers did things like parachute jumps. Mum says you wouldn't get her jumping out of an aeroplane for all the tea in China. I don't like tea so I wouldn't jump for all the tea in the world, but I probably would for a million packets of jellybeans. My Uncle Derek says he'll sponsor you for £5, and I'm going to sponsor you for £1. I haven't got any more.

I think Max in your story should be unhappy
sometimes when a big bully teases him because
he is small for his age and he can't eat what he
wants, and that's why sometimes he doesn't
want to go to school.

Love, Max

P.S. Are you jumping out of
    Christopher's plane?

Dear Max

I did it Max! I was like a jelly in a tumble drier as I sat in the plane waiting to jump. But once I was floating through the air like a gigantic dandelion seed it was brilliant, absolutely brilliant.

Love — D.J.

P.s. It wasn't Christopher's plane. He flies Jumbo jets. You can't jump out of those! He did a parachute jump as well.

30 Sharpener St
Anytown
MX 9 3BT

Dear D.J.,

Thanks for your postcard, D.J. Nobody's ever sent me a postcard before.

This is a picture of me, Mum, Uncle Derek, Pauline and Scallywag cheering from the ground as you come floating down from the sky like a giant dandelion seed, about to land in a tree.

There's a cheque for £6 from Uncle Derek with this letter – that includes £1 from me. I told my teacher Beanbrain that I was sponsoring you. All he said was, 'Jolly good. Sit down now, Max, and get ready for our spelling test'. How boring is that! Spelling is easy peasy.

Love, Max.

P.S. Your Christopher must be a brillypants pilot if he flies jumbo jets.

00-00-01
ASbank
Anytown Branch
Date 5 May
Pay D J Lucas
Six pounds only
A/c payee
£6—00
Mr D. Carle
cheque No. 000
sort code 00 0001
account no. 0001000101
This is from Uncle Derek and me.

Dear D.J.,

Jenny's definitely not my friend any more. She says I keep showing off about you. She says I'm not the same since I've been writing to you. She says I think I'm better than everyone else because I know someone famous, even though she doesn't think you are famous. I don't think I'm better than anyone else and I only talked about you because of your parachute jump and because your Christopher flies jumbo jets and because you're using my name. Now she's made it even more worse for me at school, and she says Max is a rubbish name.

It's not my fault that no one else knows anyone famous.

Love, Max

10th May

Dear Max,

Thank you so much, Max, for your £1, and please say very many thanks to Uncle Derek for me too. I raised £776 for a local children's hospital.

And thank you for your idea about Max being unhappy because he's being teased for being short. I'll have to think about that. I was teased at school because I had sticky-out teeth and a big nose. They teased me even more when I had to wear a brace. They used to call me Goofy, Fangs, Tusker, Power Schnozzle, Jumbosnout, friendly names like that. But then my face caught up with my nose and I became so much more beautiful than them that they had to stop. (Joke!)

Perhaps I could start my short story with Max being teased. Then he'll soon get the better of his teasers because he'll use his big imagination.

I'm sorry Jenny's not your friend any more and that she's made it more difficult for you at school. I think Ben sounds like a much nicer friend.

Cheer up, Max.

Love, D.J.

Dear D.J.,

I'm rubbish at writing. Rubbish, rubbish, **RUBBISH**!
Pants, pants, **PANTS**! I'm going to kill all my
characters, even Grizzle, because he's a big
cry-baby and he's useless and he
doesn't deserve to be written
about. I had to write a story
in class and I got the lowest
mark of everybody. Beanbrain
said I hadn't shown much
imagination in my writing, and
I could see Huge Bigbottom laughing.

What's your Max going to be good at? Bet he's
no good at anything. Bet he gets called
Shortypants and Tadpole and Tiddleypoo and
Titchybum. I don't think your story's going to

work. The bullies are going to win, just like they do in my class, and you won't be able to do anything about it, that's what I think.

I'm not going to write any more stories ever again. I'll still write to you though if you want me to.

Love, Max

P.S. Mr Poo wrote to Mum about the results of my tests. I've got to have an operation. I don't want to.

20th May

Dear/Max,

I wrote a story a few years ago that was turned down by *ten* publishers. I've got a drawer full of stories and ideas for stories that nobody wants.

When one of my stories is rejected, I tear my hair out, stamp round the room and shout extremely rude words. After that I think, well, perhaps that story really wasn't very good. After that I think, well, my next story is going to be so amazing the publishers will all fight over it.

I'm sure your story wasn't that bad. It probably just wasn't as good as usual and Mr Beanbrain expects more of you. So don't stop writing because of one bad mark. Perhaps Mr Beanbrain found your story too full of beans!

I must have a think about my Max and what he's going to be good at. If he's being bullied, I wonder if he will tell someone. I'm pretty certain that if my Max has to have an operation, he'll be the bravest boy on earth. What do you think?

Love, D.J.

Dear D.J.,

My story *was* bad! Ha! That surprised you.
It was truly truly bad. It wasn't my fault though.
We had to write about what we did in our
Easter holidays, and I didn't want to because
lots of people went away and we didn't. And
I wasn't allowed any eggs. So what I wrote was
boring and short because I couldn't even be
bothered to write about what we'd done,
which wasn't much.

At least you can write about anything you like.
I hate having to write about what the teacher
says. They always set such boring subjects. Next
time I have to write about myself I'm going to
make it all up. I'm going to be 6ft 6ins tall and
brilliant at football, my dad's going to be the

most famous
wildlife expert
in the whole
world, we're
going to have
a huge house
with a swimming

pool, we're going to go on lots of holidays, and
I'm going to become a world-famous author.
And my mum's going to be happy all the time
because my dad won't be dead.

Your Max will definitely be the bravest boy on
earth. I wish I was. Your Max definitely definitely
definitely won't tell anyone if he's being bullied
because he'll be too scared the bullies will find
out and make it worse for him. So there.

Love, Max

30th May

Dear D.J.,

I saw your picture in the paper! Mum showed it to me. You're really really famous. You don't look like I thought you would. I thought you would have dark hair, and I thought you would wear glasses. I can't believe the winner of the Smartstart Award writes to me. What was it like at the awards? Were you scared before you knew you'd got the prize?

If you hadn't won, I would have started a petition and got everyone to sign it. I would have gone to number ten Downing Street and protested and made the Prime Minister change the vote. And if he didn't, I would have gone to Buckingham Palace.

I wonder if anyone at school saw your picture. I showed it to Ben.

Love, Max

Dear D.J.,

I had to go and see Mr Poo today to talk about my operation. You'll never guess what. He had an *enormouse* book about bears on his desk. It had an *enormouse* photograph of a grizzly bear. Mr Poo told me that he'd seen a grizzly bear in the wild when he went to America. I told him about my story and he said it sounded very eventful and he would like to read it when I've finished it.
I told him he would have to join the queue!

It's ages and ages since I wrote to you and you

still haven't written back. Mum says it's because I make a nuisance of myself, but I thought we were friends.

What's Max doing now in your short story?

Love, Max

14th June

Dear Max,

Here I am at last. I'm sorry I haven't written before. I've been travelling around to schools, reading from my books and talking to children about writing. I told some of them about you! I said that I am helping you to write your story and that you are helping me to write mine. They were very keen to hear about the boy with the big imagination, but I said they'd have to wait until I had finished.

The Smartstart Award ceremony already seems a long time ago. Fancy your seeing my picture in the paper. It was a dreadfully nerve-wracking evening, almost as terrifying as jumping out of a plane. I had a posh frock on and when they read out my name, I nearly tripped on the stairs up to the stage because I was wearing ridiculously high heels which made me walk like a lobster. I haven't a clue what I said, but I'm sure it must have been very silly.

I'm not sure what Max is going to do in my story yet. I must think a bit more about what he is like, what makes him laugh, what makes him sad, what he is scared of (because everyone feels afraid sometimes, however brave they are), what his favourite things are, where he lives – all sorts of things. I can't really write about him until I know him properly.

Sometimes it does take a while for an idea to grow. One of my stories took three years to write and it only had 400 words!

Lots of Love, D.J.

Dear D.J.,

Does that mean I'm a bit famous now because
you talked about me to all those schoolchildren?
I wish you'd come to our school. I'm going to
ask Beanbrain to invite you. Did you tell all those
schoolchildren about Grizzle?

Did you really take three years to write a book?
How can you take three years to write 400
words? Three years is for ever and back again.
Why didn't you just give up? I would, even after
three hours. Even after one hour.

Love, Max

Dear D.J.,

This is a picture of Ritzo. He's a raccoon. Did you know that raccoons eat fish? I saw it on the telly. Ritzo hears Grizzle crying and goes to find out what's wrong. They go to the river together and Crunch is there frightening the fish away. Ritzo picks up a big stick and smashes it over Crunch's head, **WHACK!**
          WHACK!
               WHACK!
                    WHACK!,

until Crunch is nearly dead and sinks to the bottom of the river. Grizzle roars with laughter because Crunch won't be able to bully him any more. So there.

Love, Max

30th June

Whoa Max,

I can't keep up with you! Why are you so angry with Crunch? Did he really deserve such a beating? It's your story, I know, but anyone reading it might feel it's a bit violent. I'm sorry, Max, I'm only trying to be helpful. Perhaps Ritzo can teach Crunch a lesson without whacking him?

When I said it took me three years to write a story, I didn't mean that I sat at my desk every day trying to write it. I would think about it, then put it away for several months, then look at it again, then put it away again. At last, it fell into place, and I finished it and it was the best story I have ever written, even if it didn't sell millions of copies.

I didn't tell the schoolchildren about Grizzle, because he's your character and it wouldn't be right for me to talk about your characters.

Love, D.J.

Dear D.J.,

If I can't be nasty to Crunch then I'm going to
chuck him out of my story because I hate him
and he doesn't deserve to be in it. This is me
kicking him out.

And I'm going to kick Snigger out as well because
he's always laughing at me because I'm small.

People can't help it if they're small and other people shouldn't make fun of them. This is me kicking Snigger out. Good riddance to bad rubbish.

I've got to have my operation in three days' time so I won't be able to write any more of my story for ages and ages. Anyway I don't want to at the moment.

Love, Max

Dear Max

It took me a long time to find you the right card. Most of the ones I saw were soppy, naff, crass or just plain boring. I hope you like this one.

Good luck with the operation, Max. I hope Ermintrude is looking after you well and that Mr Poo does less of the insect prodding and tells you more stories about grizzly bears! I'll look forward to your next letter when you feel up to writing again.

I hope you enjoy 'My Teacher's a Nutcase', which I'm enclosing for you.

Love D.J.

Dear D.J.,

Thank you for the book and card!

I just had to write to you before I have my op.
You'll never guess what happened.
You know Mr Poo, well he saw the
book you sent me, and he said,
'Well now, Max, you're a lucky boy
having this to read. It's my son's favourite
book. In fact, he's read nearly all of D.J.
Lucas's books.' So I told him that you're
my friend, and I said, 'I bet you think D.J.
Lucas is a man', and he said that he was sure
D.J. Lucas was a man because that's what his son
had said. So I said that you were a girl and he
was amazed. Then I showed him your card, and
as soon as he read it I remembered that you

called him Mr Poo in it. Then Mr Poo looked at me over the top of his glasses and said, 'Remind me to ask Ermintrude to bring you an extra portion of flies for your lunch tomorrow'. He's  quite funny really in a scary sort of way.

My operation's at three o'clock. It's only ten o'clock so I'm going to have a read now.

Love, Max

Dear D.J.,

I don't want to be in hospital ever ever again. I hate it hate it hate it. Horrid food, horrid bed, horrid needles, horrid everything. Bet the operation doesn't do any good. I tried to stop them putting me to sleep, I kept pushing the nurse away. I wanted Trudi but she wasn't on duty. Then I saw that Mum was upset so I stopped fighting and gave in, but I stuck my tongue out at the nurse just before she stuck the needle in – serves her right.

Sometimes I feel like one of those guinea-pigs they do experiments on. And I'm fed up with not being able to eat what I want when I want.

I think I'll write a story about a guinea-pig called Shortypants that drinks a magic potion and

grows huge and takes
over the world and
makes everyone better.
All the hospitals will
be made out of sweets,
the doctors will all be

clowns and all the bad people and bullies
will be turned into toads.

The only good thing about hospital was that
Ben came to see me with his mum and they
brought me a huge box of posh biscuits.

(I bet I'm not allowed to eat them though.)
And Uncle Derek and Pauline sent me a get
well card with Scallywag's pawprint on it.

At least I get to be off school for the rest of the
term – no more Huge Bigbottom – and guess
what… Grandad and Gran are going to look
after me for a week so that Mum can go to
work. They're coming today.

How are your Max story and new book going?
I haven't written any more of my story.

Love, Max

14th July

Dear Max,

The problem with your idea of hospitals being
made out of sweets is that we'd all wind up
having to spend lots of time at the dentist's!
And if doctors were clowns they'd make
people laugh and burst their stitches. I'll go
along with bad people and bullies being
turned into toads though.

I'm sorry you had such a rotten time in
hospital. I hope you feel a bit better now.
I stayed in hospital once. The worst thing
was I couldn't get a wink of sleep; there were
so many people snoring in the beds all around
me. Rattly snores, rumbly snores, whistly

snores, croaky snores, wheezy snores – I could have started an orchestra with them and recorded 'The Snore Chorus'!

Don't worry about not writing any more of your story, Max. When I'm not in the mood, even handwashing a pile of smelly socks seems more fun than writing.

Love, D.J.

Dear D.J.,

You forgot crackly snores! You need one of
those for your orchestra! There was one next
to me. He sounded like a bonfire made of sticks!

But I'm home now and you'll never guess what
Gran did. She likes cooking but she's not very
good at it. She made some sauce but she put
too much flour in it and it went all thick and
rubbery. Grandad said we could have used it as
putty to fix the windows. I don't think Gran was
upset, but I gave her a hug just in case.

Grandad took me fishing today. It was right near
the place where I once went for a walk with
Mum. I kept expecting Grizzle to leap out and
catch a fish in front of me. And a heron flew over.

I told Grandad about Grab, the heron in my story, and how he kept snatching Grizzle's fish. Grandad says he can't wait to read my story.

We didn't catch anything, not even a tiddler. I enjoyed the bit where we put the bait on the hook, and Grandad tried to teach me how to throw the line into the water but I kept getting it caught in the bushes (I think I needed to be taller). It was a bit boring though, sitting there all day long waiting, even though Grandad tells lots of funny stories. He told me that when my dad was little they used to go fishing together, and that once my dad caught a big trout all on his own. But he hated seeing the fish wriggling on the bank so

he threw it straight back into the water.
That was because my dad always loved
animals, even fish.

Love, Max

P.S. Gran and Grandad are going
today – Boo-Hoo, except for the
cooking! Hello from Ben too!

Dear D.J.,

Guess what, D.J.... Uncle Derek and Pauline are
taking me on holiday! Mr Poo says it is all right
to go with them to Spain, on August the 12th
for a whole week. I can send you a postcard,
and I can take a friend, so I'm going to take
Ben because he's my best friend now. Mum's
going to go on a walking holiday with a friend
and Scallywag while I'm away.

How is your
short story
getting on?
I think your
Max should turn
into Superman
and beat those

bullies up **POW! POW! POW!** and turn them into ugly brown toads. Or he could turn into a giant and yell *Fee Fi Fo Fum* and grind up their bones to make his bread. Do you want me to write it for you? I've got lots of ideas. Perhaps you need a break from your story as well.

Love, Max

P.S. Are you going on holiday?

P.P.S. I've nearly finished *My Teacher's a Nutcase*, D.J. I like it when the teacher's head goes all wonky donkey and she forgets how to add up. It's really really funny, especially the bit where the wasp gets caught in the teacher's big sticky-up hair and the teacher accidentally steps into the wastepaper basket.

How do you think of things like that? I wish Beanbrain would fall into the wastepaper basket.

30th July

Dear Max,

I thought you'd like to know that a teacher at
my school *did* actually step into the wastepaper
basket! And another teacher *did* have a wasp
caught in her hair. My friend, Sally Mudge,
dug it out with a pencil. Writing books is
partly about using your imagination to make
things up, but it's also about remembering
things that have really happened and shaping
them to fit your story.

You sounded really cheerful in your last two
letters. Lucky you, going to Spain. I'm not
going away this summer because I've got to
work out the plot for my new book. My editor

is breathing down my neck like an underfed dragon and I don't like the thought of being her next meal. I'm afraid I'm spending too much time on my Max story and not enough on writing what I've already promised to do. The trouble is, I'm having too much fun thinking about Max because he is turning out to be someone rather special. Anyway, I will have to put him on a back burner for the next few weeks. So no appearance by Superman or the giant for the time being.

Have a wonderful holiday, Max. I look forward to my postcard.

Love, D.J.

Dear D.J.

We went to an amazing water park today. It had massive great slides and a huge swimming pool. Me and Ben went down this huge curly-wurley slide ten times. It was so cool. Uncle taught me how to throw a frisbee, and we had a ride on a banana boat. Uncle fell off - SPLAT!

I have written four postcards but I haven't written any more of my story. What about your book for your editor?

Love Marcos

Hello from Ben too.

D.J. Lucas
30 Pencil Drive
Writingdom

DJ1 OAU

Dear D.J.

Guess what – I'm back! I had such an amazing
time, D.J. Mum says she had a great time too.
She's much smilier since she's been back. She
says I'm brown as a berry. Ben's totally my best
friend now. He says I shouldn't let it get to me
when some people call me names. He says
they're the ones with the problem, not me.
Do you know something? His big brother died
when he was six, just like my dad died when
I was six. Ben's got three little sisters and two
of them are twins.

I think you could have a Ben in your story.
You've only got Max so far. You said that it's
difficult to write a good story with only one
character in it. I think Ben would like to be in

your story, even if he's only in it a little bit. Please, please, treble please. Are you having any bad characters?

Have you written the plot for your new book yet? What's it going to be about and do you want me to help you with it? Write soon.

Love, Max

P.S. Ben said to tell you you're his favourite author.

P.P.S. I've just had a brillypants idea. I think Max in your story should be excited because he's going to have a birthday soon.

26th August

Buenos días Max

Welcome back, and thank you for your postcard. It sounds as though you had a wonderful time in Spain. I once went to a water park in Portugal where there was a slide which began fifty feet in the air and dropped down almost vertically. I screamed all the way until I hit the water, when I fell off. It was worse than a parachute jump.

I've been working hard on my new book. The trouble is that because the weather is so good I keep wanting to go for walks with Ambush. I must tie myself to my chair and get on with it.

I think if I were at school my teacher would write 'must try harder' on my report.

Say hello to Ben for me. He sounds like a good friend, and I like him because he's chosen me as his favourite author. He's right about people who call you names. What stinkers! I'll definitely try to have a Ben in my Max story since you asked so nicely. I'm thinking of having one very bad character who scares people so much that they all pretend to be friends with him. And what a good idea for my Max to have a birthday. What do you think he would like for his birthday? I could write quite a lot about that.

When's your birthday, Max? Mine's in four weeks' time on the 19th September.

Love, D.J.

Dear D.J.,

Guess what, guess what, D.J., my birthday's
on the 18th September. I must be older than
you! When I told Mum she said, 'Well there's
a thing!' because my dad's birthday was on
the 20th September. He would have been
forty-six. Are you older or younger than
forty-six? Mum says she can't believe I'm
going to be ten.

I think more than anything else in the world the
Max in your story would like to go to a football
match on his birthday. He supports Liverpool
and he's never been to watch them, but
probably his mum won't be able to afford it,
even though she likes football as well. What do
you think?

I've got to go back to school next week. Only seven more days of holiday left. I don't want to go back. I want to be on holiday all the time.

I've got to go for a checkup now with Mr Poo. Boring.

Love, Max

P.S. I want to get on with my story again. I think I might have Grizzle going away on holiday to escape the baddies. I think he might go to Antarctica where he makes friends with the penguins and they show him how to fish underwater. This is a picture of Grizzle swimming with penguins. He looks really skinny as well as small when his fur's all wet.

30th August

Dear D.J.,

You won't believe this, but I went to see Mr Poo
for a checkup and guess what — the operation
was a success! Mr Poo wasn't wearing his glasses
and he was all friendly and patted me on the
shoulder. He told me I was a very brave boy
and he said he wished everyone was as brave
as me. Mum began to cry so I gave her a hug
and that made her worse. Mr Poo said, 'It's been
a pleasure to know you, Max, and I'd like you to
have this.' And do you know what he gave me?
He gave me his book about bears! It's so
brrrrrillypants, D.J., you should see it. Anyway, he
says that in a few weeks' time (on my birthday)
I should be able to eat what I like. **WHOOPEE!**
Mr Poo is brillypants!

Love, Max

2nd September

Dear Max,

That's great news about the operation, Max,
and well done for being such a star. I knew
you would be, just like the Max in my story. I
expect you'll start eating like a hippopotamus
when you can eat what you like.

What a coincidence our birthdays being next
to each other. I'm just a tiny bit older than
your father would have been but not quite fifty.
You're right – Max would want to go to a
football match for his birthday. I'll have to see
if I can make it happen in my story somehow.

I'm glad you've gone back to your story, Max.

At some point, you might need to look at your plot and make sure it all ties in together. That's the professional writer in me talking. The child in me just says have fun and write whatever you like.

Love, D.J.

Dear D.J.,

Even though it was my first day back at school I've got homework to do. Already!

Beanbrain isn't my teacher any more. I'm in a different class because I'm older. Did I tell you I'm the third oldest in my class even though I'm the shortest? My new teacher is called Miss Dimmer and, guess what, she's read two of your books – *Who's Afraid of the Big Bad Boy?* and *My Teacher's a Nutcase.* I told her that you're my friend. She said she hoped I wouldn't think she was a nutcase. Uncle Derek said that Dimmer is

not a very good name for a school teacher. Huge Bigbottom has already started calling her Dimbo and lots of the others are copying him, but I'm not going to. I think she likes me.

Love, Max

P.S. I was hoping Huge Bigbottom wouldn't be in my class this year, but he is. One day I'll call him Huge Bigbottom to his face and see how he likes it.

Dear D.J.,

I think Grizzle wants to stay in Antarctica for ever
with his penguin friends but he has to go back to
his river because it's too cold in Antarctica, and he
takes Splash, one of his penguin friends, with him.
When he goes back the baddies are worse than
ever because he's been away for so long. They
start to be horrible to Splash as well, just because
he's Grizzle's friend.

I think I'm going to turn
Splash into a superhero who swims
underwater and pulls Crunch down into
the water and knocks all Snigger's teeth out with
a stick so that he can't eat any more, or snigger.

I wish I didn't have to go to school.

Love, Max

9th September

Dear Max,

Oh dear, I thought you'd removed the baddies from your story, but now they're back. Poor, poor Grizzle. Perhaps he and Splash could stand up to the baddies? Do you think if they showed that they didn't care what the baddies did, then the baddies might grow bored and leave them alone?

I wonder what Miss Dimmer is like. Is she someone you can talk to, Max, if you're not enjoying school? I think if she likes *My Teacher's a Nutcase* she might just be a rather wonderful and understanding person. And that's what she's there for. I hate to think of you being miserable.

Grit your teeth, Max. Use that big imagination of yours to make things better.

Love, D.J.

Dear D.J.,

You'll never believe what happened in school today. Huge Bigbottom and his friends picked on Ben. They were horrid to him. Ben must have been upset, but he was very brave because he just stood there and glared at them. I hope they're not picking on Ben because he's my friend.

It's less than a week now till my birthday, and only a week till yours. I'm not having a party. Mum and Uncle Derek are taking me and Ben to eat at a pizza place. Did I tell you I can eat what I like now? Pasta and pizzas are my favourite things, specially pasta with creamy cheese and ham sauce. What's your favourite food?

What are you doing for your birthday? Will you have a cake? My mum bakes amazing cakes so I hope she's going to make me one.

Love, Max

Happy Birthday

A very happy birthday
on the 18th, Max
        Love from D.J.

P.s. I hope you like the
'Grizzly' card. Please
do not open the enclosed
envelope, but give it to
your mother.
THIS IS IMPORTANT!

Dear D.J.,

That was my best birthday ever! Tickets for Man U v Liverpool! How did you know I support Man U? (I told you Max in your story would support Liverpool! But I didn't tell you who I support.) You're the best, D.J. Thank you, thank you, thank you.

What a match! Did you see it on the telly? 5-2 we won. Mum and Ben (of course, I took him) and I were going nuts.

I've never seen Mum so excited. We yelled till we were hoarse. That was the best birthday present ever. Mum's sent you a thank you letter as well. And Ben's going to write to you. Everyone at school was soooooo jealous. It shut Huge Bigbottom up! And guess what, D.J.? They made an announcement over the loudspeaker that it was my birthday and everyone sang *Happy Birthday*. There was a great big *enormouse* screen and suddenly we were on it. Ben and I waved and saw ourselves waving. Uncle Derek saw us on the telly as well. I think Mum must have told them about my birthday, but she says she didn't.

This is me and Ben cheering the winning goal.

Ta ta ta ta ta ta again, D.J.

Love, Max
Age 10!

P.S. Did you see us on the telly?

P.P.S. I'm determined to finish my story
now, because I've spent ages on it already.
What's happening with your new book –
and your Max story? Did Max go to a
football match for his birthday? I don't
think you can have got very far because
you don't seem to have many ideas except
the ones I give you. I just asked Mum if it's
rude to say that and she says it is but I've
written it now so I hope you won't be
cross with me.

P.P.P.S. (*post post post scriptum!*) I'm going
to football practice at school this

afternoon and I'm going to wear my new boots that Uncle gave me for my birthday. They're blue, with red stripes on them to make me go faster, he says.

A Very
Hippy Hoppy
Birthday to you,
Daphne Jane.
        Love from Max

I hope you like my card
I did it all myself.

24th September

Dear Max,

I did see you on the television, and your
mother and Ben. Now I know what you look
like, Max. What a handsome fellow! It was
lovely to see you after writing to you for so
long and imagining what you look like.
I'm thrilled that it was such a great match.
And I didn't know that you supported
Manchester United. I guessed that you might
support Liverpool like Max in my story. It was
sheer luck that I chose Liverpool versus
Manchester United!

Thank you so much for my card, Max. It has
pride of place on my mantelpiece. I spent my

birthday with Christopher, who took me out for a delicious Indonesian meal – my favourite – and we drank pink champagne. He bought me the most beautiful necklace and earrings. My editor sent me a huge bouquet of flowers, which are sitting on my desk, and my brother is taking me to the theatre at the weekend.

I've been working on my new book while mulling over Max. Max's story, I feel, will almost write itself in the back of my mind. Then, when I sit down to put it onto paper, it will all come out in a joyful rush. I'm glad you're working hard to finish your story. I hope you'll send me a copy because I can't wait to read it.

Love, D.J.

P.S. How did football practice go?

Dear D.J.,

Did you see that programme about dinosaurs at the weekend? **WOWEE!** This is a picture of a Tyrannosaurus Rex attacking a Stegosaurus.

Love, Max

P.S. We've had three football practices and I definitely think my boots make me go faster.

Dear D.J.,

You'll never guess what. I've been picked for
the school football team! Can you believe that?
Well, I'm reserve but my games teacher says I'll
play for some of the time. Ben's in the team too.
He's really good at sport. You should see him
run. I think he's our best player.

Uncle came round with Scallywag to practise
ball skills with me. Uncle gets a bit puffed out
because he's got a great big belly (Mum says
I mustn't say that, so don't tell, please,
please, please), but he's
brillypants at juggling the
ball with his feet. He calls
himself Twinkle Toes. We
had to shut Scallywag

indoors because he kept running off with
the ball.

I've been getting really good marks for my
writing. Miss Dimmer says the stories I write
in class are all very entertaining. You wait till
she reads my Grizzle story.

Love, Max

P.S. Huge Bigbottom says there's no way I should
be in the team because I'm too small and
useless and that we're bound to lose if I'm in it,
but Ben told me to ignore him like he does.

Dear D.J.,

 You know I told you I was playing football for the school. The match was today and we won 2-0 and — guess what — I got to play for nearly all of the second half. You should have seen the faces Huge Bigbottom kept pulling. No one would have thought I would get to play for so long when it was my first match. Do you think I could be good at two things? Writing and football? Mum says I could. She says why stop at two. The funny thing is that I can't wait to get on with my story now, so I'm going to have my tea and do my homework and get started.

Love, Max

2nd November

Dear Max,

Well done, Max!

You don't know how lucky you are to be good at ball games. I'm hopeless. I was always the last one to be chosen when the other children were picking teams, and they always stuck me in goal for hockey – to keep me out of the way, I think. I can swim though, and ski. I'm just no good at hitting, catching or chasing a ball.

Your mother's right. Why stop at being good at two things? Aim high, Max!

Love, D.J.

Dear D.J.,

You just won't believe this, D.J. You just won't believe it. That big bully Huge Bigbottom went too far this time. He stood right up in front of the whole class when our teacher wasn't there, and said the most horrid things about Ben that you could ever imagine. Then he took Ben's lunchbox and trod in it. Everyone went very quiet and I was desperate for someone to say something but nobody did. So I had to do something because I looked at Ben's face and I thought he was going to cry even though he was trying not to. I stood up on a chair and I said, 'Now you listen to me, you. Don't you dare talk to Ben like that. He's just as good as you are, in fact he's a thousand times better than you are.' And then I remembered what the girl in *Who's Afraid of the Big Bad Boy?* said to the bully, and I said it to Hugo. I said, 'What made you choose today, **HUGE BIGBOTTOM**, to embarrass yourself in front of everyone!'

And do you know what happened, D.J.? Everyone started laughing at Huge Bigbottom and cheering me. Even Jenny held my hand and asked me to be her best friend again and said she hated Huge Bigbottom.

Miss Dimmer came in then and told us off for making so much noise, and she told me off for standing on a chair, and we had to get on with our lessons.

Well, at breaktime I thought Huge Bigbottom would come after me, but he didn't because everyone else came up to me and said well done. I think everyone must have been a bit scared of him even though they didn't say so and pretended to be his friend. Now no one likes him any more. That's amazing, isn't it D.J.?

This is a picture of me on a chair telling off Huge Bigbottom.

Love, Max

19th November

Dear Max,

I wish I had been there to see you up on your chair. Wow! Good for you, Max. We couldn't have that bully winning, could we? I think he'll leave you and Ben alone from now onwards.

Must fly. I want to catch the post.

Love, D.J.

Dear D.J.,

I've finished, I've finished, *I've finished my story*!
I bet you can't wait to read it. It's called *Grizzle
Beats the Dinosaurs*. Grizzle turns out to be a
great big hero when he and his best friend
Splash are attacked by a Tyrannosaurus Rex.
Mum says it's got everything but the kitchen sink
in it. You should see my picture of Grizzle
fighting the Tyrannosaurus Rex! Miss Dimmer
wants to put it on the wall of our classroom,
but I said she couldn't until Mum has made a
copy of it to send to you and one for Mr Poo.

Thank you for helping me, D.J. I bet you still
haven't finished your Max story. Tell me if you
need some more help. How old will you be if it
takes you three years?

Love, Max

2nd December

Dear Max,

Well done, Max! You did it! You're right.
I can't wait to read your story! I'm especially
intrigued by the dinosaurs which seem to have
made an unexpected appearance right at the
last minute!

You're wrong about one thing, though. I've
finished my story as well. I'm calling it
Dear Max. I've just sent it to my editor and
she really likes it. I've dedicated it to 'my
friend Max'. As soon as it's published, I'll
send you your very own copy.

Max, I'm going away soon with Christopher
to Australia and New Zealand for Christmas.

That's where I'm setting my new book – the one for my editor – and I need to do some research. We'll be away for about five weeks, so I won't be able to write to you for a while, but I promise to send you a postcard or two. When I come back, who knows, perhaps you'll be in the middle of a second blockbusting Grizzle story!

Love, D.J.

8th December

Dear D.J.,

I can't believe you've dedicated your Max story to me! Thank you, thank you, thank you, ta, ta, ta, ta!

I wonder if Grizzle could go to Australia for Christmas. He could get into a fight with a kangaroo. Did you know that kangaroos fight, just like boxers? **BIFF! BIFF! BIFF!** Funny how you don't get kangaroos anywhere else. I suppose it's too far for them to hop across the water.

I'll miss writing to you but can't wait for a postcard.

I've never had a postcard from so far away before. I'm going to surprise you by having a new Grizzle story finished by the time you get back.

Gran and Grandad and Mum and I are all going to Uncle Twinkle Toes's house for Christmas. Pauline is going to cook lunch. I can't wait. I expect Scallywag will tear up all the presents, but I like going there because Uncle's got an *enormouse* television with lots of channels and I can watch the wildlife programmes. It's going to be so much better than last year, even though I'll miss my dad.

Love to Ambush and Donut with the hole in the middle.

Love, Max

P.S. Does your story have a happy ending too? I hope it does have a happy ending.

15th December

Dear Max,

It sounds as though you're going to have the most wonderful Christmas. Say hello and Happy Christmas to your mother and all your family and friends for me. Good luck with your story if you do write one while I'm away. I'm enclosing a little something for you...

NOT TO BE OPENED TILL CHRISTMAS DAY!

Thank you for all your help, Max, and keep writing. With an imagination as big as yours, who knows where it could lead you!

Lots of Love, D.J.

P.S. Yes, my story does have a happy ending. A very happy ending.

Dear D.J.,

Before you go to Australia, I'm enclosing a little something for you, too... **NOT TO BE OPENED TILL CHRISTMAS DAY!**

And guess what,
> guess what,
>> *guess what!*

I've grown a whole six centimetres! Can you believe that? A whole six centimetres since I was last measured three months ago. And guess what as well. I'm not the shortest in my class any more. I'm only the second shortest. There's a girl shorter than me. I'm growing! I'm *growing*!

Love, Max

P.S. Thanks for the Christmas present—
I can't wait to open it! I bet you
can't wait to open yours either.